FOX BE
NIMBLE

FOX BE NIMBLE

by James Marshall

DIAL BOOKS FOR YOUNG READERS · NEW YORK

For Olivia, Nicholas, Manton, and Thacher Hurd

Published by
Dial Books for Young Readers
A Division of Penguin Books USA Inc.
375 Hudson Street
New York, New York 10014

The Dial Easy-to-Read logo is a registered trademark of
Dial Books for Young Readers,
a division of Penguin Books USA Inc., ® TM 1,162,718.

Library of Congress Cataloging in Publication Data
Marshall, James, 1942– Fox be nimble
written and illustrated by James Marshall.
p. cm.
Summary: Fox babysits for the miserable Ling children,
makes a big scene when he slips on a skate and hurts himself,
and gets to lead the band in the big parade.
ISBN 0-8037-0760-6. ISBN 0-8037-0761-4 (lib. bdg.)
[1. Foxes—Fiction.] I. Title.
PZ7.M35672Fp 1990 [E]—dc20 89-7933 CIP AC

First Edition
E
3 5 7 9 10 8 6 4 2

The art for each picture consists of an ink, pencil,
and watercolor painting, which is scanner-separated
and reproduced in full color.

Reading Level 1.9

FOX
THE
FAMOUS

Fox's mom was on the phone.

"Fox would *love* to help,"
said Mom.

"I'll send him right over."

"I won't do it," said Fox.

"Whatever it is.

I'm playing rock star."

"Mrs. Ling across the street needs you to sit with her kids," said Mom.

"Why don't *you* do it?" said Fox.

"This is my quiet time," said Mom. "Now hurry up."

"No," said Fox.

"And that is that."

"Oh really?" said Mom.

And Fox went across the street.

"How nice of you, Fox,"

said Mrs. Ling.

"Mom made me,"

said Fox.

Mrs. Ling got into her car.

"I do hope they behave," she said.

"I can handle them," said Fox.

"They're just kids."

Mrs. Ling drove off.

"Hot dog!" yelled the Ling kids.

And they went wild.

"Stop that!" cried Fox.

"Come down from there!" cried Fox.

"Quit it!" cried Fox.

"I don't have time for this!"

But the Ling kids would not quit.

They did just what they wanted.

Fox had to get tough.

"I'll tell your mom!" he said.

The Ling kids got very still.

"We'll be good," they said.

"Why don't you go play

in the backyard?" said Fox.

The kids liked that idea.

"May we play with our new balloons?"
they said.

"I don't see why not,"
said Fox.

Fox went back to playing rock star.

"The girls will love this," he said.

Suddenly he had an odd feeling.

The Ling kids were up to something.

Fox ran into the backyard.

"Come back here this minute!"

he cried.

"Bye-bye!" the Ling kids called out .

"Oh, no!" cried Fox.

"Their mom will *kill* me!

I'll have to catch them!"

He climbed the fence.

And he fell right into some mud,

tore his brand-new blue jeans,

tripped and stubbed his toe,

and ran smack into Mrs. O'Hara.

Then Fox got a bright idea.

He climbed up

to a very high place.

"I'll grab them when they float by,"

he said.

He tried not to look down.

Fox didn't like high places.

But the wind carried the Ling kids right back home.

"What have you little darlings been up to?" said Mrs. Ling. "And just *what* have you done with poor Fox?"

That night Fox's mom turned on the TV.
"A fox was rescued from a high place
today," said the newscaster.
"Why that's *you*, Fox!" said Mom.
"Fox is famous!" cried little Louise.
"Oh, quit it!" said Fox.

FOX
THE
BRAVE

Fox stepped on one of his skates
and went flying.

"Who left *that* there?" he cried.

And he landed with a bang.

Mom and Louise came running.

"I'm dying!" cried Fox.

"It's only a scratch," said Mom.

"Nothing to worry about."

"I can't look at all the blood!"
cried Fox.

"There's no blood," said Mom.

"Don't leave me!" cried Fox.

Mom and Louise put Fox to bed.

"Call Doctor Ed," said Fox.

"Before it's too late."

"Really, Fox," said Mom.

"You're making *such* a fuss."

Louise called Doctor Ed to come over.

Then she stepped on Fox's other skate,

bounced down the stairs,

flew right out the front door,

and ran smack into Mrs. O'Hara.

"Poor Louise must hurt all over,"

said Doctor Ed.

But Louise didn't cry.

She didn't complain.

Not even a peep.

"Very brave," said Doctor Ed.

"Very brave."

"Louise is tough," said Mom.

"Now then," said Doctor Ed.

"What's the matter with Fox?"

"Oh, it's just a scratch," said Fox.

"I don't like to make a fuss."

Mom didn't say a word.

FOX
ON
PARADE

"Fox is showing off!"

said Dexter.

"Quit it, Fox," said Mr. Sharp.

"We don't have time for this.

The big parade is next week."

And the band played on.

"Fox is showing off again!"

said Carmen.

"That does it!" said Mr. Sharp.

Fox was told to leave the band room.

"Come back when you have
changed your ways," said Mr. Sharp.

"But I *like* to show off,"
said Fox.

Fox sat in the school yard by himself.
"There are some things
you just *can't* change," he said.
"Look out! Look out!"
cried a voice.

Fox almost got hit.

"Oh, dear!" said his friend Raisin.

"I'm *so* clumsy!"

"You should be more careful!"
said Fox crossly.

"I'm sorry," said Raisin.

"I'm just not good at this."

"It looks easy to me," said Fox.

"Oh really?" said Raisin.

"Then *you* try it."

Fox gave the baton a twirl.

And he dropped it on his toe.

"Ouch!" he yelled.

"This is harder than it looks."

But soon he got the hang of it

and he got better and better.

Raisin couldn't believe her eyes.

"Wow!" said Dexter.

"Will you look at *that*!"

"Fox," said Mr. Sharp.

"May I speak to you a moment?"

"What now?" said Fox.

On the day of the big parade

the band was great.

Fox could show off

to his heart's content.

And the crowd went wild.

DATE DUE	BORROWER'S NAME	ROOM NO.
MAY 7 '92	Lisa H	110P
OCT 23 '92		
NOV 6 '92	Tiffay	113
DEC 9 '92	Lucreti	111
DEC 17 '92	Mallory	108
FEB 26 '93	Dylan	109
APR 1, '93	Vivien	111
MAY 13 '93	Erika	104
MAY 25 '93	Bradt	110P

20188

E
MAR

Marshall, James.

Fox be nimble.